MW00883444

DORY DILLO

MARGARET CROSS

— a friend and church member of Silver Palm United Methodist Church

DORY DILLO

© 2021, Margaret Cross.

All rights reserved. This book or any portion thereof may not be reproduced
or used in any manner whatsoever without the express written permission
of the publisher except for the use of brief quotations in a book review.

Print ISBN: 978-1-66781-1-048

CHAPTER 1

In the early light of dawn, armadillo families feasted on the ripe melons. The first crop of the season—a delicious treat!

DILLO FACT
Armadillos eat crops such as peanuts, melons, and tomatoes.

A pack of coyotes caught the dillos by surprise. No place to hide in the large open field. The young, especially, fell prey to the yelping predators. Squeals from injured armadillos pierced the air.

The killers left as quickly as they had come. The bodies of dead dillos lay scattered in the field.

DILLO FACT

The majority of armadillos
are nocturnal. They are active
at night and hide in their
burrows during the day. Natural
predators include wolves,
coyotes, bears, and bobcats.

* * *

Dory Dillo barely remembered that horrible morning. However, sometimes the flashbacks popped into her head, and she heard the sounds of the slaughter all over again.

Like now, years later, as she scurried along the narrow trail through the woods. Why had she stayed so late after school to work in the chemistry lab? She knew the dangers of being out after sunrise, but . . .

"Oops!"

Dory, startled by the bump, stumbled on a root, and almost fell to her knees.

The squeaky voice continued, "Oh, it's you—Dory Dillo, girl scientist. I'm not wearing my glasses. Have to look glamorous, you know. You're so smart. What did you invent today?"

Dory adjusted her own thick spectacles, now dangling from one ear.

DILLO FACT
Armadillos have very poor eyesight.

An airheaded cheerleader. Why did they not just leave her alone? Not every girl wanted to jump up and down and scream at the top of her lungs. No wonder they squeaked when they talked; they wore out their vocal cords from hollering. Maybe someday she could invent a magic potion and make them all disappear, but the pompom shaker still stood there squinting at her. Dory would have to use an old-fashioned way to get rid of her.

"Hi Dee Dee. No inventions today. Listen! I think I hear a coyote! We'd better get home!"

"Oh, I'm so scared!" The cheerleader scampered away.

Dory continued along the trail. Her life at school was more miserable since being selected Science Student of the Month, the first girl to receive this honor. Now everyone called her girl scientist. She knew most of them were making fun of her. Girl scientist was just another way of saying nerd.

Dory, deep in thought, walked right past the entrance to her family burrow. At least there were no witnesses to call her absentminded. She turned around and crawled through the small opening between two large gnarled roots.

"Dory, is that you?" her mother called from the kitchen.

"Yes, it's me. What are you cooking?"

"I'm trying a new recipe for termite casserole. It'll be a surprise. Did you have a good day at school?"

"Sure, Mother." Dory did not have a good day at school, but she did not want her mother to worry.

"Where's Gramps?" she asked.

"He's taking a nap in his room."

Dory breathed a sigh of relief. He was safe in the burrow. Her old grandfather moved slowly these days. She worried about him being out alone. But he liked to meet his friends at the Grub Pub, where they munched on deep-fired grubs and drank tomato juice.

"When will we eat?"

"Your father is working overtime today. We'll eat when DJ gets home from school."

Dory went into her room and shut the door. She looked at her desk: test tubes, chemistry books, a Bunsen burner—all the things she needed for her experiments. In addition, there was the abacus that her grandfather had given her. She picked up the abacus and did a few calculations just for fun.

A few minutes later, a loud thud made her jump. Test tubes rattled in their wooden rack. Dory sighed. Her brother had arrived.

"Hey, Mom. I'm home."

"So I heard, DJ. How many times have I told you not to throw down your backpack in the hallway?"

"I don't know the exact count. Maybe Dory can run it on her abacus." He looked at his sister's door. A large sign read: Keep out. Violators will be vaporized. "Maybe I'll just go in and run it myself." He started toward the door.

"Donald Joseph Dillo! You know you're not supposed to go into Dory's room!"

"Chill, Mom. Just kidding. I don't know what big secrets she's hiding. Sometimes a smell like rotten eggs comes out from under the door. And I hear strange noises. Gurgling and bubbling, even an explosion. What if she blows up the whole burrow? Besides, you and Dad and Gramps can go in."

"Dad and Gramps and I never broke her test tubes and spilled her chemicals on the floor."

"My friends just wanted to see what goes on in the Room of Weird Sounds and Smells. Well, who wants to be in there with the girl nerd—I mean scientist—anyway?"

"Don't talk about your sister that way!"

"Why do I have to be the only armadillo in the entire universe who has a sister? Why can't we be a normal family? Why can't I have three brothers instead of living with a crazy girl?"

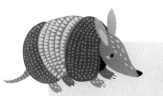

DILLO FACT
Nine-banded armadillos give birth to four identical babies, all of the same sex.

"DJ, you know why. That day the coyotes killed your brothers and Dory's parents and sisters, your father and I took in Dory to raise as our own. We wanted to create a loving family. Besides, other species have boys and girls in the same litter, and they get along together."

"My buddy, Spike, has a sister and he doesn't like her. They fight all the time."

"Well," Mother answered, "I don't know many porcupines, but I bet when they're older, they'll be the best of friends. Why don't you invite Spike over sometime? I would like to meet him."

"Okay. But I won't invite his sister."

The smell of something burning filled the burrow. "Oh, no! My casserole!" Mother Dillo hurried to the stove and took the smoldering concoction from the oven. "It's ruined. We'll have to eat leftovers."

DILLO FACT
Armadillos eat beetles, ants, termites, grub worms, berries, birds' eggs, small mammals and reptiles.

"I'll go out and look for something."

"No, you will stay inside. The sun is almost up."

"How old do I have to be before I can go out in the daytime?"

"DJ, do you have to question everything? When you have enough experience to watch for danger and to be very careful, only then may you go outside. I even worry when your father is out after sunrise. I'll be glad when he finishes digging out that new school. Maybe he can go back to working normal hours."

"Achoo! Achoo!" The old dillo sneezed as he limped into the kitchen. "What is that awful smell? Is Dory cooking up something in her lab?"

"No, Gramps," DJ replied. "Mom is trying to cook up something in the oven. See, Mom, Gramps agrees bad smells come from Dory's room. Don't you, Gramps?"

Gramps, still groggy from his nap, snapped at DJ. "Don't put words in my mouth, young man!" And then in a gentle tone, "I'm sorry, don't mind an old critter like me. What happened?"

"I'm trying a new recipe for termite casserole, and it burned. I'll just stir-fry some grubs and tomatoes and we'll be ready to eat in about fifteen minutes. DJ, put away your school stuff and get washed up."

Gramps knocked softly on the door with the warning sign. It opened, he went in, and the door quickly closed behind him. DJ tried to peek into the room, but he did not have enough time to see anything. He picked up his backpack and stomped down the hall. They always stuck together and left him out.

DJ was still in a foul mood when the family sat down to eat.

"What did you do at school today?" his mother asked.

"The usual. Math and science and other dumb subjects." He looked at his sister and stuck out his tongue.

"DJ! Stop that! If you can't behave, you'll go right to bed after we eat!"

"Ah, Mom. I want to listen to my music."

"Well then, start acting like a civilized young armadillo. Tell us about your music group at school."

DJ sighed. "As you know, I can't play the guitar like I want to. Mr. Crumker won't let armadillos play any instruments with strings. Says our claws would ruin them. Says the armadillos and turtles have to be the percussion instruments. Not *play* the percussion instruments—*be* the percussion instruments. How would you like it if someone beat out a rhythm on your back?"

Gramps peered over his spectacles. "That's why I play the harmonica. After we finish eating, I'll get it out and play some tunes."

DJ groaned. "How old-fashioned can you get? Rock bands don't use harmonicas. They'd put everybody to sleep."

"DJ!"

"Sorry, Mom. Sorry, Gramps. Sorry, Dory. Does that cover everybody? I'm going to my room."

After the door banged shut, Dory looked at her grandfather. "I'd like to hear you play, Gramps." She thought it might cheer her up. She couldn't forget about the cheerleader encounter, but said nothing. Dory seldom shared her hurt feelings with her family.

After the meal, Gramps went to get his harmonica while Dory and her mother washed the dishes. Then they joined him in the living room. Mother closed her eyes and hummed along as her father played songs she remembered from her youth. She wished her son could play the guitar. He really wanted to be in a rock band. She opened her eyes and looked at her father.

"Dad, is there any way that DJ could play the guitar? What if we let him trim his claws?"

"Matilda, you know that would leave him very vulnerable. And of course he wouldn't be able to continue on the school digging team. He likes that almost as much as his music. But . . . I'll see if I can think of something."

"Thanks, Dad. You're clever at figuring out how to do something that seems to be impossible."

"It's my training as an engineer. I like to solve problems. I'll put on my thinking cap."

Dory laughed. She pictured her grandfather wearing one of those beanie hats with a propeller spinning around on the top. She felt better when she was with him. He always encouraged her experiments. She knew she was not his real granddaughter, but she felt like she had inherited her interest in science from him. She reached over and kissed his cheek.

* * *

Soon after sunrise Father Dillo got home. "I've got bad news. The humans are going to cut down the forest across the highway and build a shopping mall."

CHAPTER 2

Mother drew a quick breath. The others sat with their mouths open. The Dillos knew many creatures who lived in the forest. They would all lose their homes. When Mother regained her voice, she said, "That's awful! Why do the humans need so many shopping malls? Those beautiful trees should be kept for all to enjoy."

The Dillo family had never actually been to the forest. Everyone knew the stories of those armadillos killed trying to cross the busy road. But to think that big noisy machines would come and knock down the trees and ruin the burrows and nests of all who lived there.

Dory recovered from the shock and decided that she would try—no, she would succeed!—in stopping this project. She would do something to discourage the humans from building on that site.

DILLO FACT

Armadillos are often seen dead along the road where they have been killed by cars and trucks during the night. When startled, their first reflex is to jump. When a car goes over them, they leap up and hit the underside of the vehicle.

The girl scientist did not sleep much that night. Her brain buzzed with ideas—maybe . . . no, that wouldn't work—maybe . . . but that would be very dangerous. She would need a lot of help from the other animals. Finally, after hours of tossing and turning, she decided that somehow an army of armadillos had to get across the highway and dig out the soil under the machines. The steel monsters would sink into the crater and the humans would not try to build on this land—maybe. She had to try. Something had to be done. She must save the forest. So many things to do, and she did not know how long before the humans would begin their destruction.

Dory had to figure out a way to get the dillos across the road without them actually walking across. She thought of her cousins who could roll up into a ball. If only her family and dillo friends could quickly roll across the street, maybe they could escape the deadly automobiles.

DILLO FACT
Only the three-banded armadillos in South America can roll completely into a ball.

No use wishing. How else? How else? Dory's weary brain finally came up with a plan: float them across the road using balloons filled with helium. Then float them back after the dig. In the dark of the night, the humans would not see the dillos at work.

Dory scribbled down some notes:

- Get balloons and helium (where?)
- Talk to the crows, raccoons (who else?)
- Recruit armadillos to dig (how many?)
- Plan for storing the balloons during the dig (helium balloons would float away if not tied down)
- Plan to get back across the highway

An exhausted Dory crept out of her room, wondering where to start on the plan. She would have to tell her family, of course, and be ready for DJ's smart remarks. And probably her parents would worry—actually, for sure, they would worry—about her being involved in such a scheme. She knew Gramps would support her from the start. That would be important, as she tried to convince the others that she had to do this.

As the family sat down to eat, Dory told them what she planned to do.

A chorus of voices rang out.

"Are you crazy?"

"Please, Dory, don't do that!"

"Too dangerous. Find another way."

Then Gramps spoke. "Of course you can do it. And I'll help in any way my old bones will allow."

After a few moments of silence, the family discussed the plan and eventually agreed to support Dory.

"I'll ask the school digging team to help," DJ volunteered.

Dory felt better. "I'll start with the problem of where to get the helium."

"Why don't you just mix it up in your chemistry lab?" DJ asked.

Dory explained, "Helium can't be mixed up. It's collected during the production of natural gas. Since we live in Texas, there are many natural gas fields, and they store a lot of helium in this area. We have to figure out how to get into the storage area and bring out some canisters of helium. We can't just go into the One-Stop Party Shop and ask them to blow up dozens of balloons."

DJ snorted. "You think they would notice that we're armadillos without a credit card? Well, I know how we can get plenty of gas for free. Just feed Gramps and his friends a lot of cabbage and follow them around collecting the output."

Dory sighed. So much for DJ's help. She would ask the other animals to assist her. The raccoons could tie the canisters to the backs of dogs—good to have friends with hands. The large dogs in the neighborhood could haul the canisters—good to have friends who were strong. She would need a place—a large place—to store all the supplies until the night of the mission. This would be the most challenging thing she had ever done.

* * *

That day at school Dory could not stay focused on her schoolwork. Her math teacher, Mrs. Brownstone, had to ask twice if Dory wanted to solve the equation on the board. How embarrassing! She could not be thinking about her plan during class.

Dory gobbled down her lunch and then got out her mission notes and thought about the strategy for getting the balloons. Humans had no problem getting their helium-filled balloons at the party shop. Her plan: after the humans had bought the balloons and tied them to the mailbox or fence to let people know the location of their birthday party, she would take them for her project. Actually, she would have to ask the raccoons to untie the balloons and the crows to take the strings in their beaks and fly with them to the storage area.

Dory had to figure out how many armadillos she would need to dig the crater, then how many balloons to lift each dillo. But first she had to experiment to find out how many balloons it would take to float one armadillo. At last the bell rang and she hurried out the door. Thankfully, no cheerleaders got in her way.

* * *

Father came home on time that morning, so Dory got to talk to him before the family sat down to eat. After listening to her plans, he shook his head. "Dory, you have taken on a challenging task. I'll help where I can, but you'll have to be the leader and get everyone to work together. By the way, I heard the clearing project will probably not begin for about a month, so that will give you some time."

Dory breathed a sigh of relief. A month would fly by, but at least she knew how long she had to prepare.

Mother called the family to the table. They dined on beetles and birds' eggs.

Father said, "Mmmmm. This is very good Mother. But why such a long time since we've had cantaloupe?"

"Because Farmer Martinez didn't plant cantaloupes this year."

"Maybe because we ate too many last year," declared DJ. "I told you we shouldn't eat the same fruit every day."

Gramps spoke up. "I'm afraid that we armadillos get the blame for eating crops when it is actually the raccoons that do the most damage. When we go into the field to eat the coon leftovers, the farmer sees us and dillos get all the blame."

"Whatever," replied DJ. "No fruit for us today."

Gramps peered over his glasses at DJ. "True, there is no fruit. But I might have some good news for you. If you can get someone to loan you a steel guitar, I know how you might play it. Just make sure it has steel strings."

"Oh, Gramps! Could you? I'll ask around tomorrow. Oh, wow! Oh, wow! Oh, wow!"

DJ was one steel guitar away from having his dream come true.

CHAPTER 3

Dory woke up feeling good. Her family supported her! Now to put the plan into action. She would ask the raccoons and crows to gather the party balloons in the neighborhood and take them to a storage area. Then she would start testing to find out how many balloons it would take to lift an armadillo. When the balloons deflated, the raccoons would untie the knot in the balloon and take off the string. She would store the deflated balloons and strings until time to inflate them with fresh helium. She would ask Father if she could use some space in the school site to store her supplies. She would start recruiting the dogs to haul the helium canisters.

DJ got home from school before Dory and threw his backpack on the floor. He hurried to find Gramps. "Gramps! Gramps! Guess what? Guess what? I have double good news. I got a steel guitar from one of my friends. His father used to play. Must be an ole timey thing. And . . . my digging team wants to help. We'll dig a tunnel under the road to get to the other side. But don't tell Dory about the tunnel. We'll surprise her."

Gramps thought to himself, not a good idea to surprise Dory that way. But he said nothing as he went to his room. When he came back with his harmonica, DJ looked puzzled. Gramps placed the guitar on the dining room table. He held down a string with the outside of one claw and then slid the flat side of the harmonica up and down the strings on the neck of the guitar. A twangy sound, unlike anything DJ had ever heard, filled the room.

Gramps smiled at the look on his grandson's face. "I think you'd better change from rock to country. I'll make a pick out of twigs. You can use it to hold down the strings. And I'll look for a piece of metal that you can use as a slide instead of the harmonica."

"Thanks . . . I think." DJ sounded doubtful as he carried the guitar and harmonica to his room.

After a while, DJ came into the living room with the steel guitar and harmonica. He wore a red bandana around his neck. "I wrote a song. Wait 'til you hear this!" The young musician played and sang:

I'm just a poor ole dillo
ain't got no grubs to eat.
How will I get my strength up
to win the diggin' meet?

The family clapped and hooted.

"Oh, Gramps, how did you know this would work? I'm going to be a star!"

Gramps looked very pleased with himself. "An old dillo knows what an old dillo knows."

CHAPTER 4

That weekend Dory's raccoon and crow friends got some balloons from a neighborhood party. She practiced launching a couple of dillos. It took more balloons than expected to get the critters off the ground. Dory made a mental note: small dillos are easier to get airborne. She now realized the raccoons and crows would have to go into many neighborhoods to get enough balloons. She hoped there would be a lot of birthdays in the next month.

DJ had his own plans for the weekend. He would lead his school team in digging a tunnel under the road. He thought this would be a better idea than Dory's plan to float armadillos across the street. But he did not know how she would feel, so he only told her about his plan as he left the burrow.

Dory, surprised and angry that DJ had not discussed his plan with her, seethed quietly. She would wait to see if it worked.

Many hours later DJ returned to the burrow covered in dirt and looking thoroughly dejected. "What happened?" Dory asked.

"Well, we dug and dug. When we came out, we were on the same side of the road as where we started."

Dory bit her tongue, thinking, these guys cannot dig a straight line. They should have spent more time studying geometry. My plan to use the balloons has to work. But she said to DJ, "You tried. Your team can help dig out around the construction machines."

"Yeah," replied her exhausted brother.

* * *

The next day, as soon as her classes ended, Dory's brain turned to plans for the mission. She wanted to focus on the project to get the helium containers. On her way home, she planned to talk with several of the dogs in her neighborhood. She knew two German shepherds and a Doberman, who seemed strong enough to carry the containers on their backs.

The canines were happy to help. When she told her family about the dogs, DJ groaned. "Not that Doberman. He looks mean. I don't trust him."

Dory replied, "His name is Brutus, and I've never had a problem with him. Besides, it might help to have a vicious-looking dog as we're breaking into the helium storage facility." She hoped an equally vicious-looking brute did not guard the facility. Then it hit her—she would be committing a crime, stealing something that did not belong to her.

"When are you going to do the helium heist?" Her father interrupted her thoughts.

"Not until the weekend. It will take us most of the night to get there. We'll hide and sleep the next day. That night we'll get the helium and start back home."

"Well, I hope you have thought this through," responded Father. "You know I have to work this weekend and can't go with you. And Gramps can't go on this kind of trip."

Gramps blinked and almost choked on his mouthful of grubs. They did not even ask him! Well, he would sure be in the group that went to the construction site. They could not stop him. He realized DJ was speaking.

". . . and I'll make sure Dory and her friends are safe."

"Thanks, DJ, but your mother and I will worry."

Mother could not speak—afraid her voice would shake too badly.

Dory did her homework and went to bed. But her sleep was disturbed by visions of snarling canines chasing her. Their teeth must have been two feet long!

CHAPTER 5

The weekend finally arrived. The small caravan left the meeting place in front of Dory's family burrow: three large dogs, five raccoons, two crows, and two armadillos. The dogs carried bundles of leashes and some dog food on their backs. Mother tearfully waved good-bye, with Gramps at her side. Father had already left for work.

The group on the ground trudged for a long time. The crows soared easily overhead. They came to a river. The dogs, with raccoons on their backs, prepared to swim across. Dory and DJ could choose one of two ways to get across: they could hold their breath and walk across the bottom of the river, or they could suck in air to inflate their stomachs and intestines and float across the water.

DILLO FACT

Armadillos can fill their stomachs
and intestines with air, and then
float or dog paddle on the surface.
Or they can hold their breath
for up to six minutes and walk
across the bottom of a river.

Dory and DJ chose the inflation method—they could keep sight of their companions. And so they each grabbed hold of the tail of a German shepherd and enjoyed an easy ride across the river.

At the first rays of dawn, they spotted the helium storage building on the horizon. They did not want to make camp too close. They found a clump of shrubbery to hide under. After unpacking the dogs, the weary travelers settled down to rest. Later, the crows could fly over the facility and check it out.

After a couple of hours, the crows left for their flyover. No one would pay any attention to a couple of birds soaring overhead. When they got back to camp, the larger bird gave his report.

"It's a small building surrounded by a chain-link fence—not electrified—and no guard tower in the yard. There's a padlock on the back door."

The raccoons smiled. One coon held out his paws. "These magic fingers can do the job."

"And I brought a piece of wire," added a second coon. "Don't worry, Dory, we'll get that lock open."

Dory relaxed a bit but still worried about digging a large enough tunnel under the fence for the armadillos, raccoons, and canisters to pass through. The dogs would wait outside the fence, and the crows would keep watch overhead.

The crows saw no security cameras outside the building. Dory supposed that this was not a high-risk storage facility, but for her little group—a dangerous challenge.

Just before sunset the crows flew again and reported that the workers seemed to have left for the day. Of course, they could not be sure there was no night guard inside. Or security cameras.

After the sun sank below the horizon, the group moved to the fence. Dory and DJ dug furiously. The raccoons cleared away the dirt. After a couple of hours of hard work, they broke through to the other side of the fence into the grassy yard. One raccoon climbed up on the back of another coon and fiddled with the padlock. Using his claws and the piece of wire, he opened the device. The worst was over—they hoped.

The coons opened the door, and with the dillos close behind, crept into the building. A small red light flashed, but DJ said it was a smoke detector—no problem. They saw stacks of boxes, but could not tell what was in them. DJ said, "I'll go check the next room." He nosed around and saw some round containers.

DJ went back to tell Dory. She followed him and went up closer to inspect the cylinders. Helium! They had found the prize! The raccoons came into the room. They did not know a helium canister from a hedgehog, but could tell Dory was excited. One coon pawed at the nearest canister, and it made a loud clattering sound as it fell to the floor. "Hush!" whispered Dory. Everyone froze. No other sounds. She took a deep breath and began selecting the smallest canisters so the load would not be too heavy for the dogs.

The raccoons wrapped a leash around each canister and dragged it outside to the yard and then through the tunnel. They used the leash to strap the canister to the back of a dog. Dory reminded them, "We have to cross the river, so please place the tops of the canisters pointing up so they don't get wet."

"Aye, aye, Captain Dory," one coon replied. "Your wish is our command."

DJ rolled his eyes. Another reminder that his sister was in charge.

With the three dogs loaded with as much weight as they could carry, the group started the long trek home, going slower this time. The dogs had to take more breaks to rest. As time passed, Dory got nervous. She did not see how they could make it before dawn. She did not want to spend another day hiding. And they had run low on food for the dogs. The other critters could forage for their meals. But as the first streaks of light appeared in the east, she knew they could not continue. Her family would be very anxious.

DJ pointed out the obvious. "It's going to be daylight soon. We're in trouble."

Dory asked the group to stop for a break. "Where are the crows?" Brutus barked sharply three times, the signal for the crows to land.

They heard the rustle of wings. "What's up?" asked one of the crows.

Dory looked at the birds and sighed. "I'm afraid we're going to have to stop for another day. Can one of you fly to my family burrow and let them know that we'll be there one night later than planned?"

The crows talked among themselves and the larger replied, "I'll go. Blackie will stay here and be your eye in the sky."

He soared away at normal speed. Flying slowly in circles over the troops on the ground had been tiresome.

The crow reached the Dillo burrow and looked for the entrance. These critters really hid their front door. He had to duck under a root into a small hole. Through the pitch black he could see a dim light ahead—something twinkling off and on and moving about. The crow approached slowly and realized the glint came from the old dillo's spectacles.

The old dillo spoke. "Who's there?"

"It's Ebenezer Crow. I went with Dory. Don't worry. They're all okay."

By this time Dory's mother had joined the old dillo. "You're sure they're all okay?"

"Yes, they're fine, and they have the helium. It's just that they couldn't make it back before daylight. They'll stay under cover and start again after dark."

The mother dillo breathed a sigh of relief. "They're okay, Gramps." She hugged him.

"Well, I'll go now," said the crow.

"Thank you so much," replied Mother Dillo.

"You're welcome," answered the crow as he slowly picked his way to the entrance of the burrow. He would be glad to get out of this dark and dusty cave. So glad he lived free in a tree.

* * *

Dory and her group started out again after sunset. They trudged along, stopping to rest when the dogs needed a break. At last, they were in their own neighborhood.

But before they went to their homes, Dory asked the dogs and coons to go to the school where her father worked and leave the canisters. His boss had given permission for them to store the supplies in an empty room. The school was close to where Dory planned to cross the street on the night of the mission. It would be a good staging area. The canisters rattled and clanked as the coons untied the precious cargo. Dory's father and several of his coworkers helped to get them safely stored.

Dory and DJ waited for their father to get off work and then walked with him back to the burrow. The young dillos were ready to collapse in their beds, but had to tell their story to Mother and Gramps before they could crash. Mother Dillo would send a note to their school to ask for an excused absence for the day they had missed.

CHAPTER 6

In the days after the helium heist, as it came to be known, Dory focused on the other items on her plan. The raccoons and crows continued to search for party balloons. In a stroke of luck, they spotted a new human housing development. Lots of balloons were displayed for the grand opening. It was like striking gold. The coons and crows worked furiously to get the clusters of balloons to the school storage site. There was not much time before the night of the mission, and Dory did not want to wait for the balloons to deflate naturally. She asked the coons to remove the strings from the inflated balloons and untie the knotted ends, releasing the helium. The sharp claws of the raccoons punctured several of the balloons. Dory sighed and hoped that she would not hear too many popping sounds. She stacked the deflated balloons in bundles of ten so she could easily count them.

Dory knew she could count on her crow and coon friends. Those who had been working with her would recruit others to help on the night of the mission. She worried about how so many coons would cross the street. The coons insisted they could run across the street and not get hit, but dead raccoons lay along the side of the road just like armadillos. However, she did not have enough balloons to lift all the raccoons that she would need.

Then a coon told her he had some friends who lived in the forest. He would ask them to help. They would not have to cross the street. He and his buddies from the helium heist would go across to train and supervise the forest coons. Dory reluctantly agreed. She could not think of a better plan. Too bad no armadillos lived in the forest.

Dory went over the mission plan again and again in her head. Helium canisters: ready. Balloons: ready. Her faithful group: ready to go. And they would supervise those new to the mission. She kept going over the numbers: armadillos, raccoons, crows. Her father, DJ, and Gramps would be there. She worried about Gramps, but she could not bear to leave him out of the mission. He so wanted to help her.

* * *

A week later Dory's father came home with the news: a piece of construction equipment appeared in the clearing at the edge of the forest. Dory thought they should perform their mission as soon as possible. It would be easier to dig around one or two machines than—who knew how many?

Dory sent word to the troops: be ready to go two nights from now. Everyone would meet at Father Dillo's work site promptly at sunset. Of course, Dory and the coons would be there earlier, filling the balloons with helium.

CHAPTER 7

And now the night of the mission. Everyone met at the school construction site and then moved to a location near the street, but somewhat hidden from passing traffic. Dory knew how many balloons it would take to lift each armadillo. She had made a list, of course.

Now she checked her notes and spoke to the raccoons. "Tie the balloons to each dillo, using one less than the number needed to fly. I will paste a piece of paper with the correct number on the back of each dillo. This way, the dillo will not take off until all are ready. When I give the word for liftoff, tie the final balloon onto each dillo."

Soon, an army of armadillos floated across the highway. As soon as a dillo got to the other side, a crow flew to its side, took the strings of the balloons in its beak, and guided the dillo to the ground. Then the coons untied the balloons and held onto the strings. The balloons had to be kept safe for the trip back across the street.

Dory told the coons how to handle the balloons. "Please tie the balloons together in clusters around some twigs and hold on to the twigs to make sure the balloons do not float away. Then take the clusters of balloons a little way into the forest to hide them."

The dillos went to work digging around the big construction machine. They would have to remove a lot of soil to get this monster to sink into the ground. The coons who were not holding the balloons helped to move away the dirt.

The dillos and coons were working at top speed when a coon came to the digging area and asked to speak to Dory.

"I'm here," she answered.

"I've got some terrible news," said the coon.

"What happened?" asked Dory, her heart in her mouth.

"When we took the balloons into the forest, they all popped," the coon responded.

Dory froze. Her brain could not process this information.

The coon continued, "There are pine trees in the forest. The needles punctured the balloons. Every balloon is flat on the ground."

Dory could not believe it. She had never seen pine trees in her neighborhood. And with her poor vision, she did not notice them mixed with the other trees in the forest. What would she do now? Her mission had become a disaster.

Finally, she recovered her voice. "I don't know how we'll get back across the street."

Gramps heard the last part of the conversation and came over to Dory. She told him what had happened. The old dillo blinked several times and cleared his throat. "This is a very serious problem. I'll try to think of another way to get us back across the street. You keep digging, Dory, and I'll work on a plan."

Dory could not keep digging. She could not focus on anything but the damaged balloons. She had to go into the forest and see for herself. She asked Gramps to go with her.

The coons stood looking at the deflated balloons on the ground. Dory and Gramps joined them. They stared at the mess. Then Gramps spoke to the coons. "Pick up all the deflated balloons and bring them out into the clearing." An idea was forming in his engineer's brain.

He continued. "Find a couple of smooth sticks about three feet long. Then tie some of the deflated balloons together end to end to make a chain about ten feet long. Put the two sticks upright in the ground about three feet apart. Then tie one end of the balloon chain to each stick."

One young coon could not stand the suspense any longer. "Why are we doing this?" he asked.

"We're building a catapult, my friend."

"A catapult?" The coon looked puzzled.

"Well, let me be less technical," responded Gramps. "You may have seen a young human boy using a thing made from a V-shaped stick and a rubber band, shooting a stone at a bird. They call it a slingshot."

"Oh, yeah." The young coon knew all about the weapon. "Sometimes they take a shot at me when I'm trying to open a garbage can."

Gramps finished the slingshot and asked Dory to select one of the smaller armadillos for a test. Dory came back with Shelly, one of DJ's digging mates. Gramps asked Shelly to back into the V-shaped balloon chain while he and Dory held it. They pulled back as far as they could, as Shelly kept backing up against the chain.

"Are you ready?" Gramps asked.

"Fire away," laughed Shelly.

Gramps and Dory let go of the balloon chain, and the young dillo shot about ten feet. "Good first test," Gramps announced. "We'll work on the catapult until you can travel far enough to get across the street." He added more balloons to the chain.

Meanwhile, the diggers had made good progress. The machine sank lower than the surrounding clearing. Of course, by now all the diggers had heard about the balloon disaster and about the new plan to use the catapult. Some were afraid of being shot across the roadway. But others, mostly the younger dillos, felt excited about traveling faster than they had ever traveled on their own four legs. Dory let the digging go on a little longer. Then she called for everyone to stop and prepare to catapult back across the street.

The coons had moved the catapult to a position along the edge of the road, out of range of the nearest streetlight. Someone had to watch for cars and trucks passing by. One crow would soar above and watch for traffic. When it looked clear from both directions, he would sound a loud "caw"—the signal to launch a dillo. The dillos lined up, ready to take their turns. Dory would go first, followed by Gramps. Father Dillo and DJ stood by to operate the catapult. Several of the crows and coons had already gone to the other side of the street to help the dillos as they came across.

At last, the moment of truth. Dory backed into the catapult and felt the tension of the balloon chain around her body. "Caw" signaled the crow. Dory shot across the street. What a weird sensation, like flying at warp speed. She landed in the gravel that bordered the roadway, digging in her claws to slow down her speed. She skidded to a stop. So far, so good.

It seemed forever before her grandfather skidded across the gravel. He could not dig in his claws to stop. He turned sideways and plowed into a tree with a horrible thud. The old dillo lay still. Dory rushed to his side.

"Gramps, are you okay?"

He moaned. "It's my leg—left front leg. Where are my glasses?"

Dory looked at the leg hanging at an awkward angle. Probably broken. She noticed a small crack in his shell on one shoulder. A coon held up his glasses: frames bent, lens shattered—Gramps would never peer through these spectacles again.

Dory had to figure out a way to get him home. Her father and DJ were across the road working the catapult. She did not know who was here and who was there. "Where's Ebenezer?" she asked.

Blackie answered, "He's across the road. Shall I go get him?"

"Yes. And please tell my father and brother what happened."

The crow flew away. In a few minutes, he returned with Ebenezer.

"Ebenezer, can you go get one of the dogs? Tell him we have to haul Gramps back to the burrow. Maybe he'll have some idea of how we can do it."

"Will do." The crow flew toward the home of the German shepherds. All was quiet in their backyard. Apparently they slept inside the house. He pecked at a window. No response.

Better try the Doberman. Good news. The big dog snored in his doghouse. The crow pecked on the roof to wake him up. Brutus grabbed his blanket in his mouth and followed Ebenezer.

When the dog and crow got back to the injured dillo, they saw the coons trying to drag him further away from the road. At this moment, DJ shot across the street. He skidded to a stop. It looked bad. He went to Dory's side. "Someone took my place on the catapult."

Dory tried to hold back the tears as she told him of her plan to drag their grandfather home. The coons had spread the dog blanket out on the ground. Dory, DJ, and several coons worked together to maneuver the old dillo onto the blanket. The coons made a harness out of some vines, tied it to the blanket, and wrapped the harness around the midsection of Brutus.

The big dog dragged the litter with the wounded dillo. With each bump in the trail, Gramps moaned. Dory's heart ached for her grandfather—she had caused his pain.

When they got back to the burrow, Mother Dillo came out, shrieked at what she saw, and hurried to her father. Dory told her what had happened. Gramps lifted his head and said in a soft voice, "Don't blame Dory. I insisted on going, and I'm glad I did. We did it! You should have seen that machine sink down! We won!"

Mother Dillo had tears in her eyes but tried to keep a smile on her face for the sake of her father. "Dad, you old dillo, you just had your last grand adventure."

* * *

When Father got home he announced, "Everyone else is okay," and then helped get Gramps into the burrow. They made a splint for his leg from a couple of twigs. DJ offered his red bandana to hold the splint in place.

At the family meal, Father Dillo declared Gramps would never again leave the burrow. He and DJ would dig out a new room next to the old dillo's bedroom. He could entertain his friends there, with Mother fixing deep-fried grubs and tomato juice just as good as the treats at the Grub Pub. Gramps did not protest. He knew that home was the only safe place for him.

CHAPTER 8

The following week in a school assembly, the principal asked Dory to come up on the stage. He announced that the developers had given up the shopping mall project and had donated the land to a conservation group to create a permanent nature preserve. They had saved the forest for both animals and humans to enjoy. He presented Dory with a scholarship to Bright Star Academy, a special school for students who had done outstanding work in their own schools. Dory would live in a dorm on campus, but could come home at school holidays.

The cheerleaders created a special cheer for Dory—quite a challenge, since they had only cheered for a boys' digging team.

Dory thanked those who had helped in the mission. When she mentioned her brother, DJ, she heard a gasp from the audience. Most of his classmates did not know that DJ had a sister. He did not talk about her, except to his closest friends. Heads turned to look at DJ. The proud brother stood up and shouted, "That's my sister!" Everyone clapped.

The assembly ended. As Dory lingered to look at her award certificates, she realized a boy moved toward her. She squinted through her spectacles but did not recognize him.

"Hi. I'm Percival."

Dory stared. She didn't know any Percival.

"I'm editor of the school paper. You can call me Percy. I'd like to interview you for an article in the paper. May I come to your burrow? I'd like to see your laboratory. And I'm also going to the Bright Star Academy. I'll be studying journalism."

Dory suddenly felt like her tongue was too big for her mouth.

"Oh . . . I . . . I . . ." A boy had never said this much to her except in the science lab. Her hands were shaking so badly that she dropped her papers on the floor. Percy helped pick them up and put them in her backpack.

"I . . . I . . . I'll check with my family." And she scurried away before she could do something stupid. But what could be more stupid than not being able to talk?

* * *

That weekend DJ came home from a digging meet and started down the hallway past Dory's room. She had replaced the warning sign with a pompom: a gift from the cheerleaders. But something was weird. Behind her slightly open door, he heard two voices—one definitely a boy. He looked at his mother. "What's going on?"

"The editor of the school paper is interviewing Dory. Get cleaned up and then come back out and you can meet him." DJ walked away, shaking his head.

When DJ heard Dory and the other voice coming from the living room, he came out of his room and walked toward the visitor. He thought to himself, his glasses are as thick as hers. What a cute couple!

Mother introduced him to Percy and then said, "I have a surprise. I found a cantaloupe in a field. I'll go get it ready to serve."

After the feast, Percy said that he should leave for home. He thanked Dory's family for their hospitality and started for the entrance of the burrow. Mother Dillo gave Dory a look and nodded her head toward the door. Dory did not move. Mother said, "Dory, please see Percy to the door."

"Oh," gulped Dory. *That* word again. She really would have to add to her vocabulary, but with Percy, the words got stuck in her throat. She followed her classmate to the door.

When Dory got back to the living room, DJ began chanting, "Dory has a boyfriend! Dory has a boyfriend!"

Dory hung her head.

Mother shot DJ her "shut your mouth" look. He shut his mouth.

Father chuckled, "Yes, Dory may have a boyfriend before you have a girlfriend, DJ. What do you think of that?"

DJ sat speechless, but only for a moment. "Well, when I get my band going, the girls will fight over me. They'll have to take a number."

Father chuckled again. "You'd better improve your sound. I don't think they'll be mooning over those twangs I've heard coming from your room."

Now DJ hung his head.

Gramps reached over and patted his shoulder. "You're getting better, DJ. Just keep practicing."

"Thanks, Gramps."

CHAPTER 9

The next several weeks buzzed with activity. Father and DJ dug out the new rec room for Gramps. Dory finished up her projects at school and sorted through her things at home. Mother fixed her daughter's favorite foods.

Finally, the day for Dory's departure. As the sun went down, her family gathered in front of their burrow. After many hugs and tears, Father, Dory, and Percy started on their way, Dory's abacus strapped to Percy's back.

Dory stopped and looked back at her family one last time. Such mixed feelings—excited to be starting a new adventure, with a new friend by her side. But sad to leave her family. She would always feel a tug at her heart when she thought of her grandfather. Then Dory turned back to the trail and took the first step toward her new life—a life where she could be proud to be a girl scientist.